For my husband, Daniel, and the two
other creatures in our house—E.J.
For Marta, Cliff, and Ella Ania—T.B.

Text copyright © 2001 by Emily Jenkins
Pictures copyright © 2001 by Tomek Bogacki
All rights reserved
Distributed in Canada by Douglas & McIntyre Ltd.
Color separations by Hong Kong Scanner Arts
Printed and bound in the United States of America by Berryville Graphics
Art direction and design by Monika Keano
First edition, 2001
10 9 8 7 6 5 4 3 2

Library of Congress Cataloging-in-Publication Data
Jenkins, Emily, 1970–
    Five creatures / Emily Jenkins; pictures by Tomek Bogacki.
        p. cm.
    "Frances Foster books"
    Summary: In words and pictures, a girl describes the three humans and two cats that
live in her house, and details some of the traits that they share.
    ISBN 0-374-32341-0
    [1. Family life—Fiction. 2. Cats—Fiction.] I. Bogacki, Tomasz, ill. II. Title.

PZ7.J4134 Fi 2001
[E]—dc21
                                                                    00-28771

FIVE CREATURES

Emily Jenkins

Pictures by Tomek Bogacki

Frances Foster Books
Farrar Straus Giroux
New York

Five creatures live in our house.

Three humans, and two cats.

Three short, and two tall.
Four grownups, and one child. (That's me!)

Three with orange hair, and two with gray.

Two with long hair, three with short.

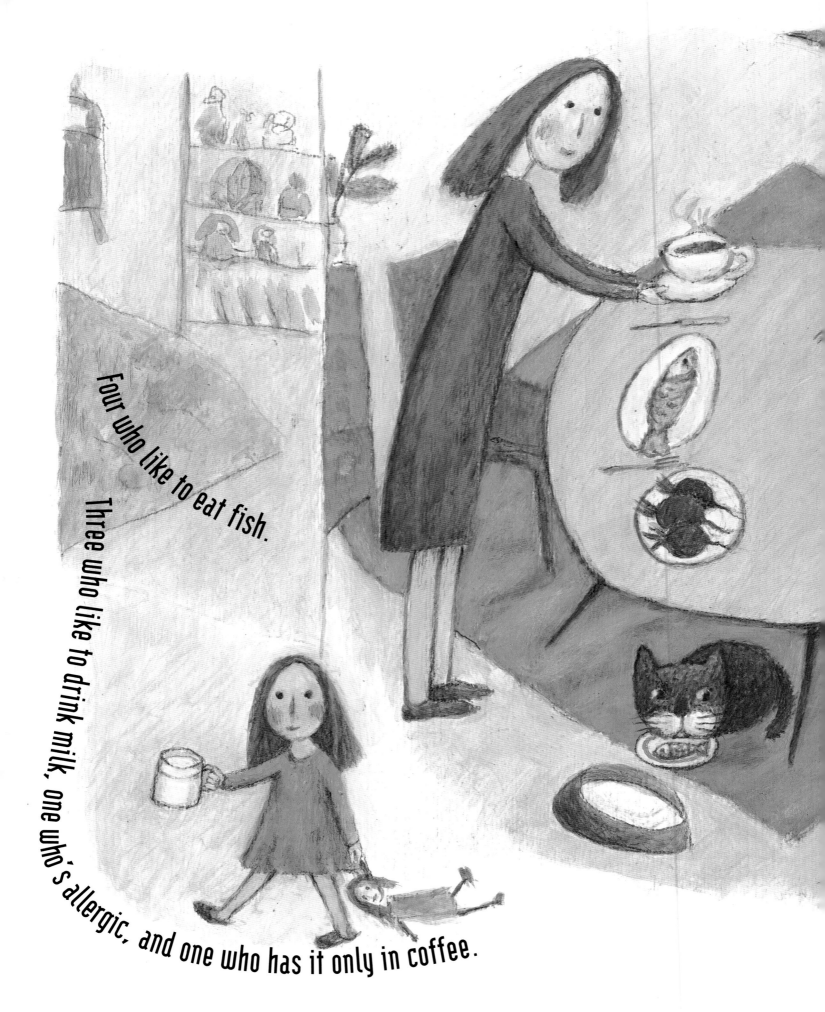

Four who like to eat fish.

Three who like to drink milk, one who's allergic, and one who has it only in coffee.

Two who like to eat mice.

Only one who likes to eat beets.

Three who sleep in my bed.

Three who don't like taking baths.

Three who can button buttons.

Four who can open cupboards.

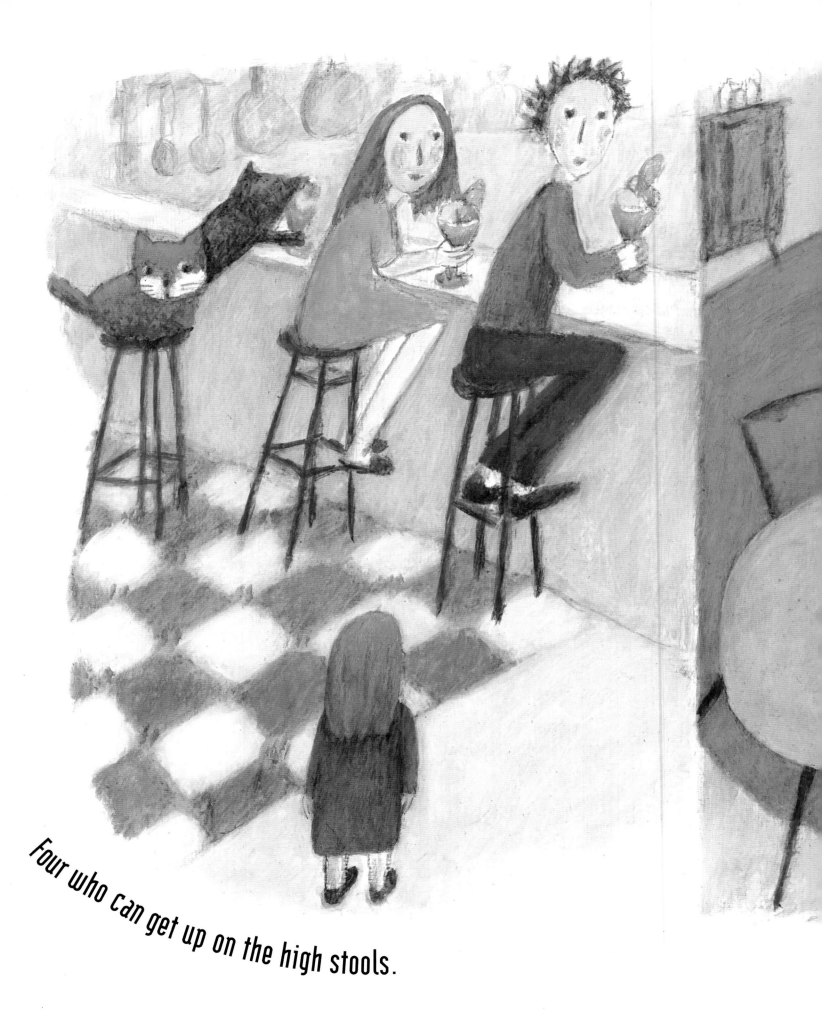

four who can get up on the high stools.

One who can crawl under the fridge.

One who sings loud late at night.

And one who sings in the morning.

Three who nap with the Sunday newspaper.

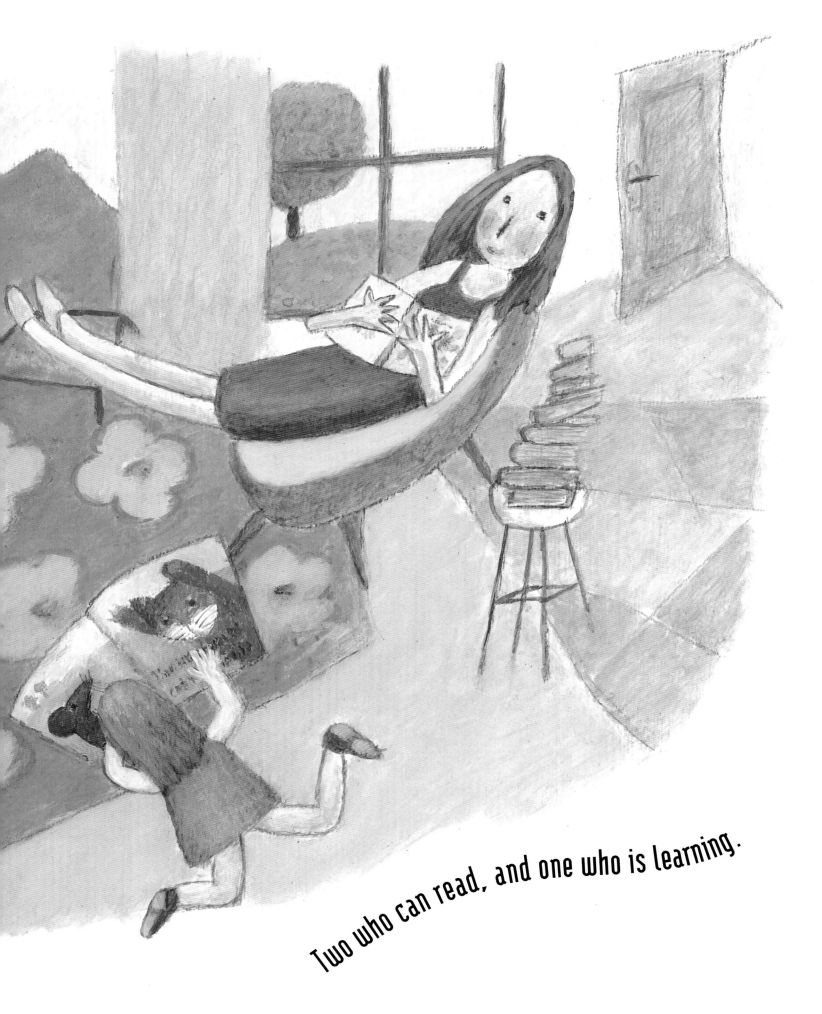

Two who can read, and one who is learning.

Three who climb trees.

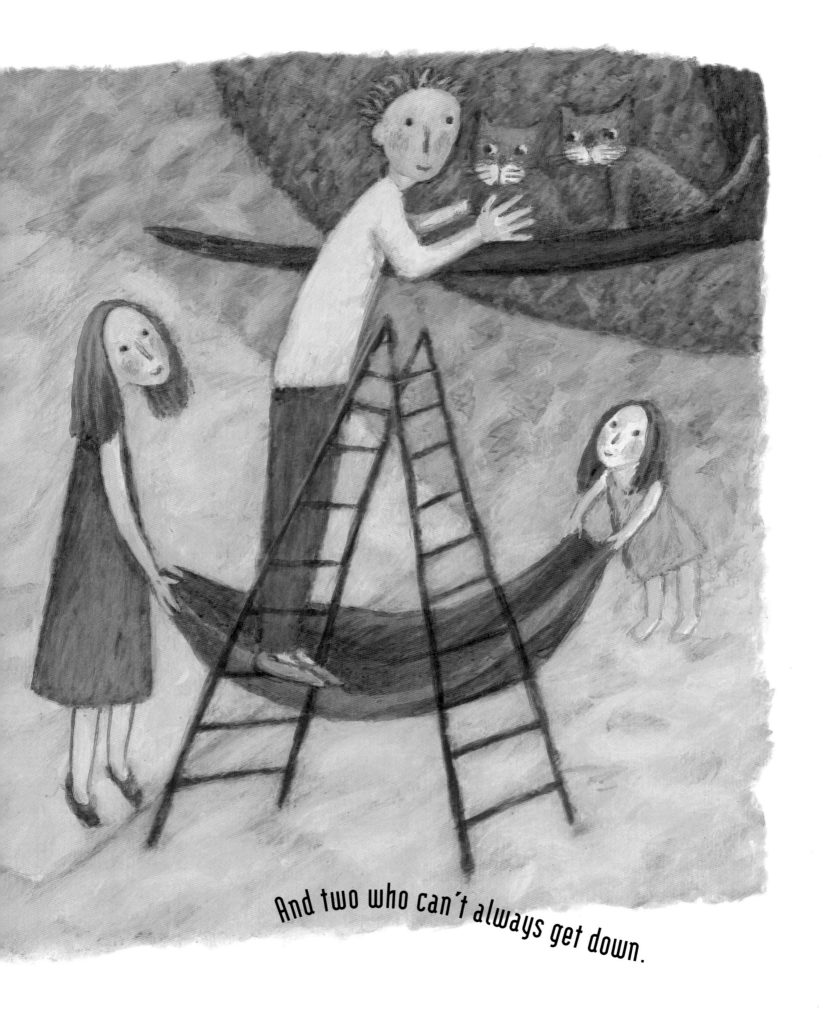

And two who can't always get down.

Five who love birds . . .

but not all in the same way.

Three who like to hide in boxes.

Four who have a knack with yarn.

Two who lick each other.

Five who kiss each other.

And five who sit together in the evening by the fire.